The Adventures of

NICHOLAS

The Adventures of
NICHOLAS

A Christmas Tale

Adapted by Helen Siiteri

Cover design by Eve Aspinwall

TRAFFORD

Canada • UK • USA • Spain

Special thanks to Kati Siiteri and Kiersten Kirkpatrick
for assistance in preparing this book for publication.

Adapted from THE LIFE AND ADVENTURES of SANTA CLAUS by Julie Lane,
published by the Santa Claus Publishing Company , Boston, in 1932

Note for Librarians: a cataloguing record for this book that includes Dewey Decimal
Classification and US Library of Congress numbers is available from the Library and Archives
of Canada. The complete cataloguing record can be obtained from their online database at:
www.collectionscanada.ca/amicus/index-e.html
ISBN 1-4120-3865-0

Printed in Victoria, BC, Canada

TRAFFORD

Offices in Canada, USA, Ireland, UK and Spain
This book was published *on-demand* in cooperation with Trafford Publishing. On-demand
publishing is a unique process and service of making a book available for retail sale
to the public taking advantage of on-demand manufacturing and Internet marketing.
On-demand publishing includes promotions, retail sales, manufacturing, order fulfilment,
accounting and collecting royalties on behalf of the author.
Book sales for North America and international:
Trafford Publishing, 6E–2333 Government St.,
Victoria, BC v8t 4p4 CANADA
phone 250 383 6864 (toll-free 1 888 232 4444)
fax 250 383 6804; email to orders@trafford.com
Book sales in Europe:
Trafford Publishing (UK) Ltd., Enterprise House, Wistaston Road Business Centre,
Wistaston Road, Crewe, Cheshire CW2 7RP UNITED KINGDOM
phone 01270 251 396 (local rate 0845 230 9601)
facsimile 01270 254 983; orders.uk@trafford.com
Order online at:
www.trafford.com/robots/04-1673.html

10 9 8 7 6 5

DEAR READERS AND STORYTELLERS

MANY are the legends and traditions that have been told about Christmas in snowy northern countries and we know how many of these legends have come to be. But *The Adventures of Nicholas* is a story such as you might tell if you wanted to combine all the warm and happy memories you like best about Christmas. I do not know of anyone called Nicholas who actually lived through these adventures, but his story is for all who believe in the spirit of Christmas.

So, draw close to the fire. I dedicate this story of Nicholas to you.

Your friend,

Helen Siiteri

CONTENTS

"He's a good lad."

NICHOLAS, THE WANDERING ORPHAN

 LONG, long time ago, in a village by the sea, there lived a young fisherman and his family—his loving wife, his small son Nicholas, and Kati, a baby girl. Their home was a little cottage built of heavy stone blocks to keep out the freezing north wind. It was a cheerful place in spite of the hardships, because all the hearts there were loving and happy.

On cold winter nights, after the fisherman had come home from his hard day's work, the little family would gather around the fireplace. Father would light his pipe and stretch his tired legs. Mother would keep a watchful eye on the two children, her knitting needles busily clicking.

One night Nicholas was trimming a tiny piece of wood with scraps from his mother's knitting, while Kati looked with wide blue eyes at the toy her brother was making for her. Mother smiled as she watched the children playing happily together. But Father shook his head saying, "I'd rather see Nicholas down at the boats with me, learning to mend a net, than fussing with little girls' toys. Now when I was his age…"

"Hush," whispered Mother. "Nicholas is hardly more than a baby himself. Time enough for him to be a fisherman when he's too old to play with his baby sister."

"True enough," said the father. "He's a good lad, and he'll be a better man for learning to be kind to little ones."

Life might have gone on in this way but for the happenings of one stormy night. Father was late, and Kati was sick with a fever. Mother knelt beside Nicholas and looked into his bright blue eyes. "Kati is very ill," she said, "and I can wait no longer for your father. I must go for the doctor myself. Sit beside your sister, Nicholas, and take care not to let the fire burn out."

Quickly kissing him, she wrapped a woolen shawl over her blond hair and went out into the bitter storm. Nicholas watched as his mother anxiously looked toward the sea for a sign of the fishing boat. Seeing nothing, she turned and walked swiftly down the windswept path.

Kati had fallen asleep. Nicholas sat beside her, dipping a cloth into a bowl of cool water and placing it on her feverish forehead, as he had seen his mother do. Slowly the hours went by. It wasn't until Kati's forehead had grown cooler, and then cold, that Nicholas allowed himself to drop off to sleep.

When the villagers found them in the morning, Nicholas was keeping watch by Kati's side. No one among them could find the courage to tell Nicholas that his baby sister had died of the fever—and that his mother had been struck by a falling tree as she was hurrying though the forest in the storm.

A few hours later they learned that the father's small fishing boat had overturned and he had drowned at sea.

Nicholas had become a homeless orphan.

THE FIRST HOME

HE kindhearted women of the village gathered at the ropemaker's house to talk about the orphan Nicholas, and what would become of him.

"Of course," said the ropemaker's wife, "the boy cannot be left to go hungry or uncared for, but we have six little ones of our own. We have taken him in only until another place can be found."

"Yes," answered plump Mistress Larsen, "but now that winter has set in, no family knows for certain when the fishing boats can go out again. We are all worried. We have so little food left."

The women shivered and drew closer to the comfortable log fire. Greta Vogel arose and looked into the fire thoughtfully. "We could take him for a while," she murmured. "We have only the three children, and Nicholas can sleep on the extra cot in the storeroom."

A sigh of relief spread through the little gathering. "But," she added quickly, "I think everyone in the village should help out with Nicholas."

"Quite right," spoke up another. "Why can't we agree that each of us here will take Nicholas for a year and then let him change to another family?"

Greta Vogel counted the women present. "There are ten of us here. If we each agree to take Nicholas for a year, that will take care of him until he's seventeen. Chances are he'll run away to sea long before that!"

The good women, having provided for Nicholas, turned their thoughts to the Christmas feast which was to be celebrated the next day.

So it was that Nicholas came to his first home-for-a-year on Christmas Eve. The kindly Vogels tried their best to help the lonely orphan. But on Christmas Day Nicholas curled up in a dark corner of the storeroom, and with heartbroken sobs mourned for his mother and father and his little sister Kati.

It wasn't long before the door opened. "What do you want?" asked Nicholas. "Go away, Otto, and leave me alone."

"My boat's broken," cried Otto, "the new boat I got for the Christmas feast. Father's gone out and Mother can't fix it."

Nicholas brushed the tears from his eyes. "Give it to me," he said. "I'll fix it for you."

"Come in here where there's more light." Otto pulled the orphan gently by the arm, and Nicholas went in where there were lights and children and laughter.

As the year passed, the little boy slowly forgot his grief in the busy, happy life of the Vogel household. Otto and his sisters played with him, quarreled with him, and came to think of him as their very own brother. Nicholas returned their love and was not too young to appreciate their kindness.

All too soon it was time to prepare for a new Christmas Day, and Nicholas knew he would have to move on to a different home and family. He wondered how he could thank the Vogels for the happy year he had spent with them.

The only things he owned were the clothes he wore, an extra coat, and the jackknife that had belonged to his father. He couldn't give any of these things away, and yet he wanted to give some small gift, especially as he was leaving on Christmas Day.

Nicholas remembered an evening long ago when he and his father had whittled small toys for Kati. "I can do it if I try," he thought. "I can make toys for them." And he worked quietly in the storeroom, using every spare minute in order to finish by Christmas morning.

The toys were finally ready. A doll for Margret, a little wobbly chair for Gretchen, and a toy sleigh with beautiful curved runners for Otto, his playmate.

On Christmas morning, as the children sadly waved good-bye, Nicholas handed the gifts to his friends. They took the little toys, shouting and dancing in surprise and happiness.

"Well, I'll be going now. Good-bye, Margret and Gretchen. Good-bye, Otto. Next year, I'll know how to make better toys. And I'll make you some *next* Christmas too." And with this promise Nicholas started out to face another year, smiling bravely, his blue eyes bright and shining in the sharp north wind.

"What do you want?" asked Nicholas.

"Well, well. A snowball fight!"

THE RACE
FOR THE SLED

N the years that followed, each Christmas Day was a happy one for Nicholas, and for all the children he met, in changing about from house to house. Nicholas did not forget his promise to the Vogels. Each year on Christmas morning he made a special trip to their house, and to every house where he had stayed, leaving gifts for the children. So it happened that each child in every family came to expect a Christmas toy from Nicholas.

As he grew into a tall, strong lad, there were many things he learned to do besides make toys. He helped the men with the boats, mended nets, and watched over the younger children for the busy mothers. The little ones followed wherever he went, and he saw that no harm came to any child in his care.

During the long winter, Nicholas went to the village school. This particular winter day, when he was fourteen years old, he heard about the race for the sled with steel runners.

"There's going to be a race on Christmas morning," Otto explained, "starting at the Squire's gate at the top of the hill. And the prize—"

"—is a big new sled with steel runners!" shouted the other boys, unable to keep quiet any longer.

"What time does the race begin?" Nicholas asked.

"Nine o'clock sharp!" The boys jumped about, pelting one another with snowballs in their excitement.

Nicholas shook his head. "I don't know whether I can be there," he said slowly. He couldn't possibly finish his chores, make the rounds with the gifts, and be on time for the start of the race. But how he longed for a chance to win the beautiful sled with steel runners!

The boys looked at him, silenced by the thought that came to every mind. Otto threw his arm around his friend's shoulders and led Nicholas away from the group. "You know you don't have to deliver those toys…" Otto began.

"But the children expect them," Nicholas whispered. "Besides, the toys are all finished."

"I mean you don't have to hand the toys to the children. Couldn't you just leave them in the doorway…early…even before they wake up?"

The two boys grinned happily at each other. "You are my best friend, Otto, but you'd better watch out for that prize. I'm going to give you a run for it!"

When the children arose on Christmas morning, they found a bright sun streaming down on the hard, crusted snow. They also found that Nicholas had been there. Every doorway was heaped with little toys, the results of a whole year's work.

After the excitement over the gifts had worn off, the villagers headed for the starting point of the race, the gate in front of the Squire's house.

Everyone, that is, except Nicholas. A runner on his little sled had broken under the weight of the wooden toys, and he was desperately trying to fix it with bits of cord and rope. Just as he made the runner secure, he heard the faint echo of the horn announcing the start of the race. He knew he could never get there in time to start with the others, but he might as well make a dash for it.

At the top of the hill, the villagers made way for him. "Come on, Nicholas, lad," shouted Jan Vogel. "Here men, let's give him a mighty good push. One…two…three…off he goes!"

Down the hill sped Nicholas, his face stinging in the swift rush of wind. On and on he went, his eyes glowing with excitement as he saw he was gaining ground on the boys ahead. Then he noticed something that puzzled him. The boys had all stopped on the other side of the frozen creek. They had hopped off their sleds and were standing quietly, waiting.

"Come on, Nicholas," shouted little Josef. "We would have waited for you at the top, but the Squire made us start when the horn blew. But you knew we'd wait for you, didn't you?"

"From now on see who waits for you," shouted Otto. "First one home wins the sled with the steel runners!" Then they were off across the fields, now coasting, now dragging their sleds, up and down hill, bumping into one another, laughing and shouting with excitement.

Nicholas was unable to speak. His friends had waited for him! They did like him even though he was an orphan, who had no home of his own and had to be passed around. His clumsy sled felt as light as his heart as he raced across the fields. It wasn't until he had crossed the brook that he realized he was leading the race.

"Up at the top of the hill there's a beautiful sled that will hold twice as many toys as this old thing," he thought. Digging his toes in the hard snow, he started back up the hill. He turned around once to see how close the others were, and heard the encouraging shouts of the villagers. Then he was at the top. He had won the race! Panting, he leaned against the big pine, and smiled and waved to the others.

The big sled with steel runners was very fine. But it was even better to see the boys who had lost the race, pulling Nicholas home on his prize. The little children hopped on behind and climbed lovingly all over him. And each mother and father smiled proudly, as though it had been their own son who had won.

"The little children hopped on and climbed lovingly all over him."

"It's a long time since I made one of these wee things."

THE NIGHT
BEFORE
CHRISTMAS

 FTER the race, the merry villagers went home to their cottages and sat down to their

Christmas dinners. But Nicholas was stopped by a tall, dark man who looked as if he

had never smiled in his life. It was Bertran Marsden, the woodcarver of the village,

known to all the children as Mad Marsden.

"You haven't forgotten that you move to my house today?" Marsden asked.

Nicholas looked at the old man. No, he had not forgotten. Nicholas knew why Marsden had offered

to take him. The woodcarver wanted a good helper, without having to pay for the work he knew he

could get out of Nicholas.

Knowing this, and thinking how lonely it would be without the sound of laughter and children's voices, Nicholas piled his few belongings on the new sled, and with a heavy heart followed Mad Marsden home.

Marsden pointed to a door in the corner of the untidy cottage. "You can put your belongings in there. As for the pretty sled, you might as well put that out in the shed. We have no time here to go romping in the snow. I'm going to make a good woodcarver of you. No time for silly toys. You'll have to earn your keep here."

Nicholas bowed his head, silently putting away his small bundle of clothes. Only the thought that he was fourteen years old, and almost a man, kept him from crying that night in his dark, cold room.

So Nicholas became an apprentice to the old woodcarver. He learned that his father's jackknife was a clumsy tool compared with the sharp knives and wheels that Marsden used. He learned to work for hours, bent over the bench beside his master, going over and over one stick of wood.

All this he grew used to in time, for he was strong and young. But he felt he could never get used to the dreadful loneliness of the place. His friends, the children, gradually gave up trying to see him after they had been chased away, time after time, by the cross old woodcarver. Marsden himself seldom spoke, except to give instructions about the work or to scold him for some mistake. Nicholas was sad and lonely and longed to be back in a friendly cottage, surrounded by laughing children.

One morning, toward the end of winter, Marsden awoke and looked about the room in surprise.

Nicholas had swept and scrubbed the floor, had taken down the dirty hangings from the windows, and was busily polishing the pots and pans with clean sand. The table was set in front of the fire and a shining copper kettle was bubbling on the hearth.

Nicholas poured boiling water over the tea leaves, spread some bread with fresh, sweet butter, and said simply, "Your breakfast, Master." From then on the cottage began to look less like a workshop and more like a home.

One night, as Marsden sat in front of the fire silently smoking his long pipe, he saw that Nicholas was still bent over the workbench. "Here, lad," he said almost kindly. "I'm not such a hard master that I make you work night as well as day. What's that you're doing?"

Nicholas answered quickly. "It's just a piece of wood you threw away, Master. I thought I'd see if I could copy that fine chair you're making for the Squire's son. It's a…toy," he explained fearfully.

Instead of flying into his usual rage, Marsden said, "Here, let me see it." With a few skillful turns of the knife, the old woodcarver finished the toy to perfection. Then instead of handing the little chair back to Nicholas, he held it in his hands with a sad expression on his worn and wrinkled face.

"It's a long time since I made one of these," he murmured. "Yet I made plenty, years and years ago, when they were little."

"When who were little, Master?"

Marsden's eyes grew fierce and angry. "My sons," he roared. "I had two sons, and when they were as big as you are, they left me. Ran away to sea. Left me all alone to grow old and crabbed." The old man buried his face in his hands.

Nicholas went over and placed his strong hands on the bent old shoulders. "I won't leave you," he whispered.

Marsden lifted his head, "You're a good lad, Nicholas. I think I'd like to help you with some of those little things you make. We'll make them together these long winter evenings, eh Nicholas? And you won't ever leave me alone, will you, lad?"

The boy answered quietly, "No, Master. I'll stay with you just as long as you want me."

So every evening the two heads bent over the workbench. With help from the master, the toys were more beautiful than they had ever been before. The dolls' cheeks were as rosy as the little girls who would soon hold them in their arms. The little chairs and tables were stained the same soft colors as Marsden used on his own furniture, and the boats and sleighs were shiny with bright new paints.

The night before Christmas everything was finished. A toy for each child in the village was packed in the sled with the steel runners. Yet Nicholas and the old man were still working at the bench. They were trying to finish a chest which had been ordered by a wealthy woman in the next village, twenty miles away.

The chest had to be finished and delivered on Christmas Day. It was a wedding present, and the Christmas feast would also celebrate the wedding. Nicholas would have to borrow a horse and sleigh, and drive over with the chest early Christmas morning—the time he had planned to take the gifts to the children.

"I'm sorry, Nicholas," said old Marsden. "I'd go myself, but I'm not as strong as I used to be. It's an all-day trip—twenty miles over, several hours to rest the horse, and twenty miles back. With the snow not crusted, it will be hard going."

"If only she didn't want the chest on Christmas morning," sighed Nicholas.

"Well," answered his master, "we did promise it and it has to be delivered. Now the toys weren't promised—"

"No, but I've always given them," interrupted Nicholas.

"I was just going to say, lad, that they weren't promised for Christmas Day. Now, you know that little children go to bed early. Why can't you…"

"Of course!" cried Nicholas. "I can deliver the gifts tonight, after the children have gone to bed. Why, Master, that's a wonderful idea!"

The old man and the boy rushed around and finally got the sled out in the yard. Nicholas bundled himself up and was off through the snow, dragging the toy-laden sled behind him.

Down in the village, a bright winter moon was shining on snow that glistened on rooftops and around the doorways. Not a soul stirred in the streets but one young boy, going from door to door, leaving a pile of little toys every place he stopped, until there was nothing left on the sled.

It was Christmas Eve, and Nicholas had once more kept his promise to the children.

There was a funny object seen dangling outside the door.

THE FIRST
CHRISTMAS
STOCKING

HE old woodcarver cheerfully taught Nicholas all that he knew of his difficult trade. The years went by busily and happily, and for Bertran Marsden they were the happiest of his life. When old age finally overcame him and he passed away peacefully in his sleep, the old woodcarver gratefully left his cottage, his tools, and his thriving business to Nicholas, whom he loved as his own son.

As Nicholas himself grew older, the sound of children's voices grew dearer and dearer to him. He arranged his work so that he spent only part of his time on the orders he received; the rest of the day and most of the evenings he worked on toys for the next Christmas. One Christmas Eve he was surprised to find that the children had hung on their doors little embroidered bags filled with oats for his horse. After that, instead of leaving the toys piled up in the doorway, he put them in the little bags. He now had a long list of children to remember, for he made a point of noticing which families had new babies and of finding out about newcomers who came to the village.

So it was that he knew all about Jon and Peter. Their mother and father were even poorer than most of the other families. The father had been strong and able before his boat was smashed in a storm and he was so badly injured that he had to lie in bed or be propped up in a chair in the cottage.

The neighbors gave the family as much as they could spare, and the mother worked whenever she was needed in the Squire's house on the hill. But there were many days when the children had only a bowl of thin porridge to eat, and the mother and father went without anything at all.

Jon was now the man of the family, although he was only eight years old. He built the fire, shoveled snow from the cottage doorway, and took care of his little brother while his mother was out working. One of his chores was going into the forest and helping the woodcutter, a kind man, who paid him with enough wood to keep the family from freezing during the long bitter winter.

One cold winter afternoon, as Jon was returning from the forest with his sled piled high with wood, he met a group of boys who were building a snow fort close by Nicholas' cottage.

"Jon!" called out one of the boys, "want to be on our side?"

"I guess not," he answered, "I have to get this wood home before dark."

"We'll help you with your sled if you stay a while," the boys promised.

Jon hesitated, then dropped the rope to his sled and joined the group. It was a long time since he had played in the snow, and he braved the icy sting of the snowballs and finally climbed the slippery walls of the fort, pelting snowballs down on those trying to defend it.

Suddenly a glad shout rose from both sides as Nicholas appeared, his blue eyes twinkling at the sight of everyone having such a good time.

"Help us, Nicholas," pleaded the boys who were trying to take the fort.

Nicholas quickly gathered up a handful of snow, packing and shaping it in his hands, and taking aim at the tallest boy, knocked his hat clean off. The boys rushed forward, and with Nicholas shouting them on, they captured the fort!

Jon looked at the tall man shyly. Of course he knew who Nicholas was; he had heard about the woodcarver ever since they had moved into the village last summer.

As the group started to break up and the boys gathered around Jon's heavy sled, Nicholas looked down and smiled. "Is this a new boy in the village?"

"Yes, his name is Jon and he has a little brother, Peter...and his father is paralyzed and can't work," a young boy called out. Jon's face turned white, and with a desperate tug at the heavy sled he hurried down the snowy path.

One of the older boys cried, "Now you've done it! You've hurt his feelings by talking out like that. I'm going after him…"

They ran after Jon, leaving Nicholas smiling with sympathy and understanding.

When the boys caught up with Jon, they tried to make him forget the thoughtless remark by talking about the man they had just left. "Every Christmas since I can remember," one boy began, "Nicholas has left gifts at every door in the village."

"Not every door," corrected another. "He only leaves toys at the doors where he sees an embroidered bag. We put oats in it for his horse, and it shows Nicholas that children live there."

How jolly and kind Nicholas had looked, Jon thought. It would be wonderful for his little brother Peter to have a gift on Christmas Day. He didn't care about himself, but for Peter's sake he must do his best to try to find a bag.

That night Jon spoke to his mother. "Do you suppose we have a bag in the house?" he asked.

"What kind of bag, child?" she asked in surprise.

"Well, it should be an embroidered bag, but I guess any kind would be all right. You hang it outside the door on Christmas Eve, and Nicholas the woodcarver knows there's a child inside and leaves a toy."

The tired mother sighed. "Things like potatoes and flour come in bags, child, and those are things we haven't seen for many days. It sounds like nonsense, anyway. I've never heard of anyone who gave away toys to poor children, and I'm sure this Nicholas doesn't either."

But Jon was not able to forget about Nicholas. He thought of how happy and excited his friends in the village sounded when they talked about the woodcarver. Nicholas wouldn't pass by a child's house just because he was poor — not if he saw a bag hanging outside.

By Christmas Eve, however, Jon had just about given up hope. There was no way of finding or even making a bag in time. As he made a neat pile of little Peter's clothing, he picked up a long, woolen stocking and said jokingly, "Now this could hold a gift just as well as any old embroidered bag…"

"Jon!" little Peter cried. "Why are you staring at my stocking? What are you going to do with it?"

"Do with it?" Jon shouted. "I'm going to hang it outside the door!"

Much later that evening, Nicholas, laughing silently and chuckling to himself, filled the stocking right up to the top with enough toys to make two little boys very happy. The next morning, young Peter, reaching down into the toe, found five large pieces of gold, enough to keep the whole family comfortable through the winter. The mother's eyes were bright with happy tears, and the father almost sat up in excitement.

But it was Jon who hugged close to his heart the very first Christmas stocking.

"I'm not as fat as I might be."

HIS FIRST RED SUIT

QUIRE Kenson, the richest man in the village, came driving up to Nicholas' cottage one day with an order to carve a new chest for his youngest daughter, who was planning to be married. Nicholas heard the sound of silver bells and reindeer hoofs on the snow, and when he opened his cottage door he saw a shiny red sleigh drawn by two beautiful reindeer. They were called Donder and Blitzen—thunder and lightning—because they traveled so swiftly.

While Nicholas was listening to the Squire's directions about the size of the chest, he was secretly admiring the fine suit of red deerskin his visitor was wearing. As he made a note of the instructions, he missed no detail of the Squire's outfit: the short coat belted at the waist, and the trousers tucked into shiny boots. Soft white ermine trimmed the collar, cuffs, and the bottom edge of the coat. A warm red hat, also trimmed with the expensive fur, fitted closely over his ears.

Long after the Squire had driven off behind the flying hoofs of Donder and Blitzen, Nicholas' thoughts were still on the beautiful red suit. "There's no reason why I can't have one too," he thought to himself. "I have all my winter supplies, and the wood for the shop is paid for. And there is still a bag of gold coins left over that I will never be able to spend. The Widow Aspen can make good use of the coins. They say she is very clever with a needle. I think I'll drive over there and see what can be done. I've gone around looking like a poor orphan, instead of a prosperous woodcarver, long enough."

So Nicholas hitched up his old horse, who was getting slower and slower as the years went by, and paid a visit to the Widow Aspen.

"I want a fine red suit," he explained. "You know the one the Squire wears?" The woman nodded. "Well, I can't afford to have all that deerskin dressed and prepared, and I know very well I can't have mine trimmed with real ermine. Now what could you suggest?"

The widow thought a moment. "Well, we could get a good piece of homespun from the weaver, and I could dye it myself. I have a wonderful red dye made from boiling the red rowanberries. And I'm sure we could find enough white rabbit skins to trim the coat. It would make a fine suit, Nicholas."

Nicholas took a handful of gold coins out of his pocket and laid them on the table. "There," he said, "I think that will be enough to take care of the material and labor."

"But…but Nicholas, it's more than enough," the widow gasped. "Why half of this would keep my family all through the winter."

"Then keep it," Nicholas answered gently. "You've had a hard time, since your good husband died, to keep your little family warm and well fed. I have enough to spare, so let's not quibble over a few gold coins. I'll not be the man to die with a fortune hidden under his mattress."

The widow stood at the door and watched Nicholas drive away through the snow. "There's a fine man," she murmured, letting the gold pieces jingle through her fingers. "A fine big man."

So she bought the homespun and dyed the cloth a beautiful bright red.

And then a strange thing happened. Nicholas could spare no time from his work to have a fitting, so the widow cut and sewed the suit with the thought of a fine big man guiding her hand. Nicholas was not a short man by any means, but he was rather thin, and yet as Mistress Aspen pieced the suit together she knew she was sewing for a big, generous man, and she made the suit to fit Nicholas' heart instead of his body.

When at last the suit was ready, Nicholas arrived to try it on. The widow gave one look and burst into tears. "Oh, Nicholas, I've spoiled it, I've spoiled it! I thought you were bigger. Whatever made me cut it so wide? Whatever shall I do?"

Trying to comfort the woman, Nicholas forgot his own disappointment. "There, we won't worry about it. It's only that I'm not as fat as I might be. Why, if I ate all the food that the villagers send me, I'd fill out this coat in no time. The trousers will be all right as soon as I buy a pair of boots to stuff them in. And what a fine cap this is! See how close it fits? Why, the whole outfit will keep me warm and comfortable!"

To show her that he was pleased with the suit, he insisted on wearing it home and sat up high on the seat of his sleigh, ignoring the stares and giggles of the villagers.

When he arrived home, however, he sat down in the huge suit and burst out laughing. "What a sight I'll make going around like this. Yet I'll have to wear it out, it wouldn't be right to waste good material. There's only one thing to be done. I'm too thin for my height, so I'll just have to eat more meat and potatoes, and drink more milk."

So Nicholas kept his big red suit and paid more attention to his meals. His face became full and rosy, his chest filled out, his arms and legs grew more muscular, and he even began to develop— whisper it—a round little belly!

"I shall really have to eat oatmeal in the morning."

Everyone ran about in a frenzy

DONDER
AND
BLITZEN

NE Christmas Eve, Nicholas found to his dismay that the children had followed Peter's example of putting out a woolen stocking. Some families had five or more children, and there was often a row of stockings nailed up on the door. Nicholas couldn't very well put in just one toy—the stockings looked so flat and empty. But by giving each child several, Nicholas soon found he was all out of toys, and only halfway through his list!

"Lucky I have that extra supply at home in the chest," he said to himself as he made a flying trip back to the cottage. He loaded up his sleigh again and started out once more, with the night half gone and the list still not completed.

Poor old Gunnar, his horse, tried his best, but he could not make much headway through the heavy snow. He kept turning a weary head around to Nicholas, who urged him on. "Come on now, Gunnar, only two more houses. You can make it; the sleigh is not so heavy now." Gunnar bravely dug in, trying to budge the clumsy old sleigh, but his worn-out old legs collapsed. Down he went, sending the sleigh into the nearest snowdrift. Nicholas climbed down, and after making sure that Gunnar had no broken bones, he shook his head. "Looks as though we'll have to get a new sleigh, and I'm afraid your traveling days are over, too."

For many days after that the villagers noticed that Nicholas was not working at his bench. Instead, they could hear sounds of hammering and sawing from the large shed where he built furniture and other big pieces.

Spring came, and Nicholas was back at his workbench. When Otto, his old friend, came to ask what he had worked on so secretly all winter, Nicholas only shook his head.

"You'll see soon enough. What's this I hear about the Squire?" he asked Otto, to change the subject.

"Ah," said Otto, puffing his long pipe, and settling down for a piece of gossip. "They say things haven't gone so well with the Squire these past years. Now he has to sell most of his land and household goods to pay the bills and move to a village to the south, where the winter won't be so hard on his old bones. Will you be going up to the sale tomorrow, Nicholas?"

"Now what would I be buying from the Squire? I don't want any more land, and I myself can make as fine furniture as any he has in his house."

"He has some good animals up there—two fine horses and that set of reindeer."

Nicholas, finally interested, put down his hammer. "Gunnar's too old to be much help to me now. I think I might go up and take a look around after all."

So the next morning Nicholas wandered down to the Squire's stables and was surrounded by a group of men. They thought he was interested in buying a horse, and they were willing to give him plenty of free advice.

Nicholas, however, walked past the stables where the horses were, and went directly to the larger stalls.

"He's after Donder and Blitzen," the men whispered. "He's always admired them—they go so fast."

Two reindeer, excited by the noises of the crowd, poked their frightened heads through the top part of the door.

"Well," said Nicholas softly, "you don't look much like thunder and lightening now. Not afraid of me, are you?" The deer whimpered and thrust their warm black noses into Nicholas' hands. "I guess we'll get along all right. Now to find your master and see about this sale."

The Squire, a bent old man with a worried look on his face, seemed dazed by the mob of people buying up his house and goods. "Well, you can't have Donder and Blitzen alone," he said. "That set of reindeer goes together or not at all. Why, Donder would go raving mad if you tried to separate her from the rest of her family."

"Family!" exclaimed Nicholas. "Why, I need only two reindeer. How many more are there?"

Suddenly there was a loud crash of breaking wood, a mad rush of people away from one of the stalls, and a brown streak went running about the farmyard chasing one unfortunate man who couldn't run as fast as the others.

"That's Vixen," shouted the Squire. "Catch him quickly. He's a young imp…he may hurt somebody!"

Everybody ran about in a frenzy, but Vixen was nimble and even paused to look over his shoulder and shake his head as if to say, "Come on, catch me!" Then he was off, leaping over carts as he skillfully dodged his pursuers. He knocked a man's hat off with his young horns that were just beginning to grow, and finally cleared a high fence, only to stop and turn, and look calmly back at the breathless men on the other side.

Nicholas had not joined in the chase. He was holding his sides, shaking all over with laughter. "I'll take the lot of them," he cried out. "I don't know what the others are like, but I must have that Vixen! I haven't laughed so much in years."

So it was that Nicholas acquired not two but eight reindeer: Donder and Blitzen, the mamma and papa, and their six children, Dasher and Dancer, Comet and Cupid, and Prancer and Vixen.

THE NAUGHTY REINDEER

 N order to shelter his eight reindeer, Nicholas had to build an extra shed that was almost as large as the cottage itself. All went well as long as the animals stayed where they belonged, but Vixen delighted in butting his head against the door of his stall, so that Nicholas had to rebuild it three times. He would hear a loud crash and look up from his work with a sigh. "I suppose that's Vixen again. Now if he were only as quiet and gentle as his brothers…but I don't suppose I'd like him as well."

Vixen wanted to be as close to Nicholas as possible, and would break down one door after another in order to caper up to the cottage and leap around until his friend noticed him.

Nicholas tried to be severe. "Now this time you'll be punished! I have too much work to do to bother chasing you around."

But the little reindeer only treated it as a game, and would hide behind a tree, poking his head around the trunk and almost laughing at Nicholas as he tried to catch him.

Nicholas worked night and day to finish the toys. He scrubbed and curried the reindeer until their hides were sleek and shining. Finally the great night arrived. Nicholas made many trips back and forth to the woodshed, his arms loaded with bright little dolls, houses, boats, and animals. He opened the stall where his reindeer were waiting and led them out into the yard.

"Donder and Blitzen in the lead," he said, "Then Dasher and Dancer because they're next strongest, and then Comet and Cupid, and then Prancer and…why where's Vixen?"

Nicholas dashed into the stable calling, "Vixen! Vixen, you young imp, where are you? If I catch you I'll…"

Suddenly there was a noise on the cottage roof. Nicholas looked up and saw Vixen playfully butting the chimney with his horns.

"You bad reindeer! How did you get up there?" Nicholas shouted, really angry now, for he would have no trifling with his Christmas visits to the children. "And how are you going to get down, hey? I'll tell you: you won't get down. I'm through with you. I'll leave Prancer at home and take only six reindeer."

Vixen was really sorry now, and he was really frightened. So frightened that he couldn't remember clearly how he had reached the roof. He looked down at Nicholas, who turned away and began to harness the other reindeer.

Vixen became annoyed. How dare they leave without him! He stamped an angry little hoof on the hard crust of the snow. Crack went the crust, and Vixen felt himself sliding down the slope—swiftly, swiftly, and right over the edge, only to land in a soft snowbank right at Nicholas' feet. Nicholas began to laugh, and it was a meek and ashamed little reindeer who took his place quietly beside Prancer.

Nicholas then opened the woodshed door and revealed a most beautiful sight. There stood a bright, shining red sleigh, the runner curving up in front to form a swan's neck, the back roomy enough to hold toys for a whole village full of children.

It had taken him most of the long winter to get everything ready, but as he climbed up on the high seat, beautifully padded with soft cushions, he knew it was worth his hard work. He took out a long shiny black whip, snapped it in the air, and they were off!

The villagers were awakened from their sleep by the merry jingling of silver bells, the stamp of reindeer hoofs on the packed snow, and the snap of a whip in the quiet air. They peeked out from behind their curtains and saw a splendid sight.

They saw in the moonlight a new red sleigh drawn by eight prancing reindeer, traveling like lightning through the deserted streets. Traveling so fast that they wouldn't have believed they had seen it if they had not recognized the familiar figure high up on the seat.

As they returned to their warm beds, they murmured, "That's Nicholas on his way to the children. God bless him!"

"If gold's all you care for, here's more."

NICHOLAS FINDS A WAY

NE year, when Nicholas was about sixty years old and his beard had grown as fluffy and white as new-fallen snow, a strange family came to live in the village. It wasn't much of a family to be sure—just a little old man, as brown and as hard as a nut, and one little thin girl who shrank away from the crowd of villagers who gathered, as they always gathered, when something new was happening.

"His name is Karl Dinsler," one woman whispered. "They say he's very rich, and so he must be, to have money enough to buy the big house on the hill."

"He may be rich," sniffed another, "but he certainly doesn't look it. Did you see how shabbily he was dressed? And that poor little thing he had with him looks as if a good meal wouldn't do her any harm. Who is she anyway?"

"That's his granddaughter. The child's parents died a short time ago, and they say this old man bought the house up here to be alone."

"He can stay alone then," remarked another. "Did you see how he scowled at us when all we wanted to do was welcome them to the village?"

"Yes, but somehow I pity that little girl. Who will take care of her up in that big barn of a place?"

It was lucky the villagers had a chance to get a good look at the newcomers that first day, because after that, little was seen of them. The girl seemed to have vanished completely, and the old man came down from the hill only to buy small amounts of food—some fish and some flour.

It was the schoolmaster who told the villagers of the strange thing that had happened. "He's nailed up all the gates except the front one, and that he keeps locked with a heavy bolt. Besides that, he's put boards on all the windows and even on the front door. When I tried to ask if he planned to send the child to school, he wouldn't let me past the front gate."

"Well, at least the little girl will make some friends at the schoolhouse," one mother remarked.

"I'm afraid not," the schoolmaster replied. "When I told him that the children usually brought in vegetables or a few coins to pay for their schooling, he told me to go about my business—that he'd take care of his grandchild's education."

"Why, the man must be crazy!" the villagers said, astounded. "He must be afraid of something."

"Afraid, nothing," one man exclaimed, "unless he's afraid someone will take his gold away from him."

"Well, this news will interest Nicholas," said another. "One more child in the village, and a lonely one too."

"Nicholas knows all about her," they heard a deep voice say, and they all turned to see that it was the woodcarver himself. "Her name is Kati. I once knew a little girl named Kati," he went on, a sad look in his usually merry blue eyes. "And that is why I'd like to do something for this poor child."

"Why, how did you find out her name, Nicholas?"

"She was wandering around in the yard, and I stopped to talk to her. She says she's not allowed to go outside the fence and that she can play in the yard only an hour each day. She also told me her grandfather doesn't want her to play with the village children, for fear she'll talk about the gold he has."

The honest villagers were indignant. "As if we'd touch his old money," they said angrily.

"I don't know what we can do about it," said Nicholas. "We can't force our way into the house, and after all, she's his own grandchild. We'll have to wait and see what happens. I can't believe anyone could stay as mean as that with a little child."

The others shook their heads. "He's mean all right. Why he probably won't even let her put out her stocking on Christmas Eve."

Nicholas laughed. "No, he wouldn't open his front door even to get something free."

However, Nicholas carefully made a few little toys for Kati and packed them away with his other gifts. Just about a week before Christmas, when he was looking up at the dark, boarded-up house, hoping to catch a glimpse of Kati, a wonderful idea struck him. His eyes brightened and he chuckled to himself. "I'll try it, by golly, I'll try it! I may get stuck, but it's worth the try."

DOWN THE CHIMNEY

 CHRISTMAS Eve that year was a dark, moonless night. The wind whistled through the deserted streets, and a cold sleet stung Nicholas' face and covered his sleigh with a shining coat of ice.

"Come on now, my good lads," he encouraged his reindeer. "The trip's almost over; we've only the house on the hill now." He tied the deer to the front gate and stopped to listen. Not a sound could be heard but a few shutters banging in the wind and the sighing of the big pines.

Nicholas crept over to the side of the house where there was a porch with a railing. There it was easy to reach the roof. Stout as he was, he leaped nimbly to the top of the porch, and in a few moments was crouched on the sloping roof of the house.

Now came the dangerous part. The roof was slippery where the sleet and rain had fallen. Nicholas had to take out his little knife and hack away the ice to get a foothold. Once he paused when he thought he heard footsteps in the darkness below, but it was only Donder stamping impatiently in the bitter cold.

Finally a big shape loomed up above him: it was the chimney. Nicholas peered down into the inky blackness. "Just as I thought," he murmured. "The old miser lets his fire go out at night."

He climbed over the edge, feeling carefully with his feet; and bracing his back firmly against the walls, he slowly made his way down the sooty chimney until he felt solid ground beneath his feet. When his eyes became used to the darkness, he found the stub of a candle and lit it. Then he set to work swiftly.

From his pocket he took a gay red stocking which he filled to the top with little toys and nuts and raisins; he thought the hungry little girl might like a few sweets. Then he hung the fat stocking from the mantel of the fireplace, weighting it down with a heavy candlestick. He was just leaning over to blow the candle out when Karl Dinsler flung open the door and burst into the room.

"Sneaking into my house, eh? After my gold, I suppose. I'll show you how I treat thieves, I'll show you!" The old man picked up a heavy pair of fire tongs and made a furious lunge at Nicholas, who quickly stepped aside so that the table was between him and the mad old miser.

"Don't be such a fool, man," Nicholas said quickly, realizing the danger he was in. "I haven't come here after your gold."

"Then what brings you here? Why do you break into an honest man's house in the dead of night if it isn't to steal the gold I'm supposed to have?"

"Look behind you at that stocking there. The other children in the village leave theirs outside their doors, but Kati is too frightened to ask you for anything. I wanted her to find gifts on Christmas morning, the same as the other children do."

The old man looked at the stocking, bursting with toys and goodies, and slowly lowered the fire tongs.

"You give things away?" he asked, unable to believe what he had heard.

"Yes," answered Nicholas, "I'll even give you a Christmas gift. If gold's all you care for, here's more…and more…and more to add to your hoard." He reached into his deep pockets and poured a stream of bright gold on the table under Karl's astonished eyes.

"That's just to show you how unimportant I think money is compared to the love of a little child. Do you ever see Kati's eyes twinkle at you, or do you only see the bright glitter of this stuff? Do you ever feel the warmth of her little hand tucked into yours, or are you satisfied with the cold touch of gold? I feel sorry for you, old man, but don't you touch that stocking or I'll make you feel sorry for yourself as well. And now," he finished indignantly, "I don't intend to climb back up that chimney. Kindly show me the way to the door." He marched out of the room, covered with soot from head to toe, and old Karl hurried ahead of him to let him out into the black, stormy night.

During the following week the village buzzed with excitement. Something had stirred up the old miser on the hill! He had ripped off the boards from the doors and windows, and had sent for the schoolmaster. Within a few days Kati and her grandfather walked down the road to the school, the little girl's face beaming up at the old man and her warm little hand tucked in his.

It was many, many months before the villagers discovered it was all because Nicholas had climbed down a chimney to fill a little girl's stocking!

"And these are our Christmas Trees."

THE FIRST
CHRISTMAS TREE

ERY close to Nicholas' cottage was a thick grove of pine trees—tall, beautiful, dark-green trees that lifted their branches high up into the sky and made a perfect shelter on the ground beneath. Scattered in among the larger trees were little firs, which stayed green all through the cold winter.

The children loved to play in this grove because, no matter how stormy the weather, this spot was always warm and sheltered. And in the summertime it was a delightful place, with the sharp scent of the pine trees and the soft murmuring of their branches in the breeze.

Nicholas loved this little grove too because in order to get there the children had to pass his cottage, and they would often dash in to talk for a while with their old friend.

One wintry day toward the end of the year, Nicholas looked out of his cottage window and saw a group of children running for dear life away from the grove. At first he thought it was some sort of game, but then he saw that something must have frightened them. A few of the smaller ones were crying, and they didn't stop running until they had reached the cottage.

"Why, now, what's all this?" Nicholas asked, picking up the littlest fellow and trying to comfort him. "All you big boys look so frightened! Come inside and tell me all about it."

"We were playing robbers in the pine grove and it was my turn to hide, so I could jump out at the others," Arno, the oldest began. Nicholas nodded his head.

"Well," the boy went on, "I saw the trees move a little and thought it was the others, so I shouted, 'Robbers!' and jumped out and…and…"

"And it wasn't us at all," shrieked little Elsa, sobbing. "It was somebody else hiding in the woods."

Elsa's older sister explained. "We heard Arno shout 'Robbers!' so we ran out too, and saw a man with long black hair and a terrible mustache with gold rings in his ears. He looked at us and said something we couldn't understand, so we turned around and started to run."

"Then," said Arno, "we ran right into more people who looked like him—lots more—and even women and babies. Bad men don't go around with babies, do they Nicholas?"

"No, I expect not," Nicholas said, smiling. "And just because people look different doesn't make them bad. Besides, I think I know who they may be. Did they have any horses or carts with them?"

"They had three or four horses and a big covered wagon. One of the wheels had come off, and it looked as though it was stuck in the snow. Who are they, Nicholas?"

"Do you know, I think they might be Gypsies," said Nicholas.

"Gypsies!" exclaimed all the children at once.

"Gypsies don't usually come this far north in the wintertime, but these people may have lost their way, and they can't go farther south now until spring comes. Very few travelers can get through the pass in the mountains, and if their horses are old they would be foolish to try."

"But where will they live, Nicholas?" Elsa asked, no longer afraid. "The little babies and their mothers can't stay out in the cold, and there aren't any houses in the village where they can stay."

Nicholas shook his head. "That's true, but I guess Gypsies are used to all kinds of weather. Why, I'll bet those babies would cry if they woke up at night and saw a real roof over their heads."

"I'd like to camp out in the open all the time like the Gypsies," said one of the boys who had been most frightened. "Only, how can they hang up their stockings if they have no doors?"

"They haven't even got a chimney. Even Kati's house had a chimney," said a little girl. "Do you think they like toys, Nicholas? Are they like other children?"

"Yes, those little Gypsies out there in the pine grove are just like you," Nicholas said, whistling for Vixen to come play with the little group. So the children forgot their fright and started to play robbers with the little reindeer, who was a splendid playmate because he always wanted to do the chasing.

Just as Nicholas had supposed, the band of Gypsies had been caught in an early winter storm. They explained their troubles to the villagers, who gave them as much food as they could spare, but there was no hope of anyone having enough room to offer them shelter. The Gypsies would just have to make the best of it in their wagon and tents in the pine grove, relying on the thick evergreens to keep out the winter winds.

The children soon made friends with the Gypsies, and there were many happy times in the camp. The Gypsy fathers would build big fires, and then all of them would gather around to sing their sad, sweet songs. Toward Christmas, the village children entertained the Gypsies with long stories about Nicholas—how he went around from house to house filling stockings with beautiful toys and sweets and nuts, and how he even went down a chimney one Christmas Eve because there was no other way of getting into the house.

The Gypsy children listened eagerly. But then they looked at the ragged tents where they lived and shook their heads. "He couldn't visit us," they said. "We have no doors, no chimneys, and we never wear stockings."

Little Elsa, who wanted everybody to be happy, reported these things to Nicholas. Although he never said anything, she knew that the smile on his lips meant he had a plan in his wise old head.

Christmas Eve finally arrived. But this year, after he had finished going to each house in the village, Nicholas drove his reindeer right past his cottage and out into the forest. He stopped at the pine grove, where he was met by Grinka, the Gypsy leader.

"Here are the candles, Grinka. Remember what I said you're to do?" The man nodded. "Good! You do your part and I'll follow along with these things."

The Gypsy silently went from one little fir tree to another, twisting a piece of cord around the base of each candle and tying it to a branch. Then Nicholas would finish decorating the tree with shiny red apples, brown nuts, and, of course, his lovely hand-carved toys. There were over ten of the evergreens to be trimmed, as Nicholas insisted on having a tree for every family of Gypsy children. It was almost dawn before they finished.

"Now for the lights," said Nicholas.

They went quickly from tree to tree, touching a taper to each candle, until the whole grove was twinkling and glowing with warmth and beauty.

"Be sure to waken the children before the sun shines through the pine trees and spoils the effect," Nicholas warned.

"All right," said Grinka. "I'll go and wake them now, before you go."

"Oh no!" said Nicholas in alarm. "They mustn't see me. The children must never see me. Now I must go."

A few moments later Grinka aroused all the children in the camp. They danced around among the beautiful trees, each one discovering something to exclaim about.

"It's the lights that make everything so beautiful," said one child.

"Oh no, it's the gifts!" shouted another.

"It's the fruit and sweets," added one hungry youngster, who was stuffing his mouth with goodies.

"I think everything is beautiful because it's Christmas," decided one wise boy.

"Yes, yes, because it's Christmas," they all shouted, dancing around. "And these are our Christmas trees!"

The light inside the forest grew dimmer and dimmer.

A PRESENT
FOR NICHOLAS

OLVIG—or Holly, as she was called—was one of those timid little girls who hated to go to bed, not just because it was bedtime, but because she was afraid of the dark. She was a lonely little girl too, because she was also afraid of the other children. Some of the big boys in the village used to tease her by making loud noises behind her back and jumping out at her from dark corners. So most of the time she played by herself or kept busy raising her flowers.

"Flowers!" her father would exclaim in disgust. "We have them in the yard in the summer and then she putters over those flower pots in the house all winter. Why she's afraid of almost every living thing in the world except flowers. Silliness, I call it."

"Some day," her mother would say, "something will happen to make Holly forget her fears. She's such a good child, she'd do anything for someone she loved, even if it took the last ounce of her courage."

Holly loved flowers, and she had wonderful skill in raising them in the harsh northern climate. The little garden around the cottage was lovely all through the short summer. Then, when the first sharp frost of the autumn chilled the air, she would tenderly transplant all the plants which would grow in the house, and gather seeds from the others for spring planting.

Like all the other children of the village, she hung her stocking on the door every Christmas Eve, and every Christmas morning discovered the same lovely gifts and sweets. But unlike the other children, she couldn't take for granted the warm generosity of Nicholas, the woodcarver. She wanted to show him how thankful she was that someone did not think her odd because she was afraid and shy with other children.

She thought and thought of something to do that would please Nicholas. Finally she decided that she would give him something that gave her more pleasure than anything else in the world: she would share her flowers with him.

So, the little girl picked a small bouquet of bright blossoms from her window boxes, bundled up in her cloak and hood, and started for Nicholas' cottage. "I'm glad he lives at the edge of the wood," she thought to herself as she walked down the road through the deep snow. "I don't think I could ever make myself walk into the woods." She shivered and walked a little faster, holding the fragile bouquet close to her warm cheek to protect it from the cold.

"I'd like so much to talk to him," she said to herself "I'm sure he doesn't know me. They say he's getting so old now that he doesn't remember all the children and just fills a stocking wherever he sees one. I think I'll just leave the flowers outside the door, the way he leaves his gifts. That's what I'll do," she decided, and skipped along until she reached the cottage gate.

She crept quietly across the yard and was just about to leave her posies on the doorstep when a loud crash from the stable made her freeze in her tracks. Her heart almost stopped beating, and she was too terrified to move. A huge animal burst through the open stable door and rushed straight for her.

She shut her eyes and thought wildly, "I'm going to die!" A moment that seemed like a year passed, while she waited silently for death. Then, finding that she was still alive, she slowly opened her blue eyes and stared straight into a pair of beautiful soft brown ones.

"Oh, it's a reindeer," she gasped, losing some of her fear. But she was still too frightened to move.

Vixen, growing tired of standing still, moved closer and closer until his nose touched the pretty flowers. He opened his mouth and nibbled one. It tasted so good he began to eat another.

Holly angrily snatched her flowers away and began to pound Vixen with her closed fist.

Suddenly she heard a voice behind her say, "Here, here! What are you doing to my Vixen?

You're frightening him!"

She turned and saw Nicholas standing in the doorway. "I frightened him!" gasped Holly.

"Yes, of course you did," said Nicholas. "Don't you know deer are timid creatures and easily frightened?"

"But he was eating your flowers and…do you really mean to say he was frightened of me?"

Nicholas laughed a little impatiently. "Yes. My goodness, child, didn't you think you could frighten an animal like that?"

"No," said Holly softly. "I've never scared anybody in my life. Somebody's always frightening me."

Nicholas looked down at the pale little face. "Come into my workshop and let's talk a while," he said quietly. "I think we shall have to get acquainted."

After Holly had been served a bowl of warm milk, Nicholas asked, "What is your name, my dear?"

"Holvig is my real name, but everyone calls me Holly. I came to bring you flowers, but…but… Vixen ate them." She looked shyly at Nicholas, and they both burst out laughing at the thought of the naughty little reindeer.

Nicholas wanted to know all about Holly's garden and her winter plants and her family. As the little girl talked, the kindly woodcarver realized how lonely and fearful she was.

"Well, I think you did a very brave thing to save my bouquet," he said when she had finished.

"But I was really afraid at first," Holly said truthfully.

"Perhaps you were, Holly. But to do something when you're really afraid is braver than if you don't feel any fear at all. Always remember that, my dear."

"I will, Nicholas," she promised, "and I'll bring you some more flowers next week."

As Holly left the cottage, she noticed Vixen poking his head at her from behind a tree. Her heart skipped a little, but she straightened her shoulders and walked over to the reindeer.

"Boo!" said Holly to Vixen. Vixen turned and ran.

HOLLY
GETS ITS NAME

 OLLY often brought a bouquet of her flowers to Nicholas, and she and the woodcarver soon became very good friends. Nicholas would sit at his bench working on his little toys, and Holly would sit on a stool at his feet and talk and talk. She discovered that talking about her fears here in this cozy room somehow made them seem less frightening.

One time he asked, "Are you afraid of rabbits, Holly?"

"Oh no!" she laughed. "That's one thing I know that's afraid of me. Why, rabbits even run at my shadow!"

"True, they are fearful little creatures," said Nicholas. "Did you ever see where rabbits live, Holly?"

"Yes, they go down into little holes in the ground, don't they?"

"Mmmmm," answered Nicholas, busily carving. "They must be terribly dark, those little holes. Yet those little timid animals go down there to bed every night and probably don't think anything about it."

Holly frowned. "I see what you mean, Nicholas. If my room were really as dark as a rabbit's hole, maybe I wouldn't mind. But it's only half dark, and the chairs and table and things look so different in the moonlight. I…I sometimes think they are goblins."

"You little silly," said Nicholas tenderly. "Now you listen to me. We're friends, aren't we?"

Holly nodded and climbed up on his knee.

"Well, I'm going to tell you something. There aren't any goblins, and there aren't any terrible creatures who run around trying to harm little children. If you're a good girl and do what your mother tells you, and say your prayers before you go to bed every night, nothing can harm you. Do you hear me? Nothing."

Holly looked very much impressed. "It will be hard at first," she said after a moment. "But if I think I see a goblin in my room, I'll just say, 'Nicholas says you really aren't there!'"

They both laughed, and Nicholas told her it was time to run home to her supper.

Spring arrived, but just when it was time for planting, Holly became ill with fever. All through the short summer weeks she lay on her bed, not recognizing anyone, not even her beloved Nicholas.

He took flowers to her, hoping they might bring back her wandering little mind, but she only pushed them away. In her illness, Holly screamed about big black giants and horrible goblins, and Nicholas sadly realized that all their friendly little talks had been completely wiped from her mind.

Many months later, Holly recovered. The fever had left her the same timid little girl she had been when she first brought a bouquet to Nicholas. Now she sat at the window during the day and stared out at the bare, cold little yard. It was winter again, but this year there were no flowers.

Holly was lonelier than she had ever been during her entire life. For long months to come she would have nothing to bring to Nicholas. She pressed her thin little face against the windowpane and looked with tear-filled eyes out into the bleak front yard.

Two boys were passing the gate and stopped to wave kindly at her. Holly waved back and wiped her eyes. She pushed open the window and called out, "What's that green stuff you have under your arm, Peter?"

The boys came over to the window. Peter held up an armful of lovely red berries scattered among shiny, pointed green leaves.

"We got it in the woods…way back in the part they call the Black Forest. It grows like this all through the winter," Peter told her. "I don't know what the name of it is."

"Here," said Eric, "you can have a little branch of mine if you want. I'd give it all to you," he added shyly, "except I don't think we'll be going back there, do you, Peter?"

"I wouldn't go back there alone, I can tell you. If you got lost there, I guess you'd stay lost."

The two boys went on their way, leaving Holly a small branch of shiny green leaves and bright-red berries. The cheery plant somehow reminded her of Nicholas, so bright and rosy. But the Black Forest!

Holly buried her face in her hands. "If only I dared to do it," she sobbed. "But even the boys are afraid to go there alone. Nicholas said that to do a thing when you're really afraid is braver than if you feel no fear at all. But I can't go, I can't!"

She sat there for a long time, trying to decide what to do. "I've got to do it...for Nicholas...I haven't any flowers for him. But it's a horrible place...something terrible will happen to me. No— Nicholas said nothing could harm a good child, and I've tried to be good. I think...yes, I'm going to do it!"

Holly ran for her cloak before she had a chance to change her mind and before her mother returned from the village.

Nicholas looked up from his work and saw a little girl running along the road, right past his cottage and into the woods. "That looks like Holly," he thought in alarm. "No, it can't be. She's not well yet, and besides, she would never have the courage to go into the woods. It must be some other child."

An hour later, however, Holly's mother knocked anxiously on his door. "Oh, I thought she was here," she said worriedly. "Where has she gone? She's lost, and it's beginning to storm!"

Nicholas was quickly pulling on his bright-red coat and stocking cap. "I'll find her, don't you worry." He looked out at the gray afternoon sky. The air was filled with millions of snowflakes blowing in every direction, striking fear in the hearts of the man and woman who knew that Holly had to be found before darkness closed off the woods.

"I know where to look," said Nicholas. "I'll take the small sled and Vixen. You sit down here and make yourself comfortable, and I'll have your Holly back before the snow covers my front walk."

Holly, meanwhile, had found the tree with the red berries, and had stayed longer than she intended, to gather a huge armful of the branches. By the time she started back, the snow had begun to fall.

"I can't understand it," she murmured, as she tried to find the narrow path. "It's getting darker and darker." She began to run, her head bent against the wind, her feet tripping over the rocks and stumps hidden in the snow.

"I can't see anything," she sobbed. "I can't lift my feet any more." Panic-stricken, she saw a huge shape coming at her through the clouds of snow. She closed her eyes and fell face down in front of Nicholas and Vixen.

When she awoke, she was in the woodcarver's cottage. Her mother was holding her in her arms, and Nicholas' kind face was bent over her.

"Where are the branches?" she asked. "I went into the Black Forest alone to get them for you. Where are they?"

Nicholas put the bright leaves and berries in her arms. "Here they are, my dear. Did you bring them for me?"

"Yes, Nicholas. I was afraid, but I never will be again. I know that now."

Nicholas wiped a tear from his eyes. "You shouldn't have gone out so soon after you were sick. But I love the plant. What is it called?"

"I don't know, but I like it because it reminded me of you. The berries are so round and red and shiny," Holly said, beginning to smile.

"That's funny," answered Nicholas, "it reminds me of you. It's so brave, growing out there in the cold, and the little berries have the blood-red of courage in them. So I know just what we should call your plant. From now on, we'll call it 'Holly.'"

The old head drooped drowsily.

THE LAST STOCKING

 HE years went by, and Nicholas grew to be a prosperous old man. But as his good deeds increased, his strength and vitality ebbed slowly away. The villagers, who loved and respected him as they would a saint, grew sad when their children played happily with their toys on Christmas morning. The fearful thought in every parent's heart was: "Maybe next Christmas he won't be with us."

One year a group of men and women called on Nicholas at his cottage with a suggestion. "We've been thinking," said Otto, Nicholas' old friend. "It's too cold for you to stand and fill each stocking outside the door. Couldn't the children leave their stockings inside, by the fireplace?"

"Then you could come in and get warm, and take your time," said one woman kindly.

Nicholas raised his white head from the work he was always doing, and a smile spread all over his rosy face. "The idea of your coming here to tell me how to do my work," he joked. "Why, I remember filling embroidered bags for some of you when you were younger than your own children are now. Then they started putting out stockings instead of bags, and now they're going to put the stockings in by the fire. Well, times change, I suppose, and I must keep up with the times. So indoors I will go, and I thank you all for your warm fires."

That Christmas Eve old Nicholas found it more and more difficult to leave each fireplace for the next house. The warm blaze made him drowsy, and his old bones ached as he pulled himself up wearily to be on with his work.

When he reached the last house, Nicholas found that the children had left a cup of warm chocolate and a few cookies for him beside their stockings on the fireplace. Nicholas chuckled and sat down to enjoy his snack. The old head drooped drowsily, and soon he was fast asleep.

He awoke with a start an hour later when the anxious father gently shook him by the shoulder. "Are you all right, Nicholas? I got up to see if the fire had gone out and found you still here. Look, it's almost dawn!"

Nicholas shook himself and stood up wearily. "Yes, it's Christmas morning and I haven't finished my work," he said sorrowfully, looking at the empty stockings.

"I'll do it for you," answered the man. "You just leave the toys here and go home to bed. Go along now, before the children get up and see you."

Nicholas smiled gratefully and went out into the gray dawn.

A few minutes later a little boy stood in the doorway of the living room. "Why are you filling the stockings, Father!" Christian asked, looking ready to cry. "I thought is was Nicholas who gave us the toys!"

His father tried to explain. "Nicholas is getting old, Chris," he said. "Sometimes we parents have to help him. But don't you forget it's always Nicholas who leaves you the toys."

"That's all right then," said the little fellow. "It isn't so much fun if you think of Christmas without Nicholas."

It was almost noon, and Holly, as she did every Christmas morning, was on her way to decorate Nicholas' cottage with the bright leaves and berries that bore her name. She quickened her steps when she noticed there was no smoke coming from the chimney.

"Poor old dear," she thought. "He's probably all tired out from his trip last night. I'll just go in and make his fire and put the holly around."

She went into the cold, silent cottage and soon had a warm blaze crackling on the hearth. Quietly, not to disturb Nicholas' sleep, she decked the walls and windows with gay branches. There was one sprig of holly left over. She couldn't find a single bare spot left in the room, so she decided to take it into Nicholas and place it on his pillow.

Opening the bedroom door quietly, she saw him lying there, still dressed in the bright red suit with the white fur and the shiny black boots.

"Here's your holly," she whispered, bending over Nicholas. How still he was—too still. She dropped the holly and sprang back.

"Nicholas, Nicholas!" she screamed. She ran out into the snow, stumbled blindly down the road to the village, and with tears streaming down her face call loudly for the townsfolk.

They gathered in little groups to listen to her story. The bells tolled, and the village was in darkness that Christmas night. Vixen and his brothers whimpered in their stalls, and the bright holly lay beside the quiet figure in a red suit.

THE SPIRIT
OF CHRISTMAS

 HE villagers tenderly put Nicholas to rest in the pine grove, close to the spot where the children came to play. The reindeer were no longer in the stalls behind the cottage; they had been taken up to the big stables on top of the hill by Kati Dinsler, who put them out to pasture and cared for them in loving remembrance of her old friend.

Many a time during the sad year that followed, a mother would pick up a little carved toy and, with tearful eyes, silently remember the generous heart that had given the gift.

But as time passed, Nicholas might very well have been forgotten if it had not been for the children. "Are we going to hang up our stockings this Christmas?" was asked in every household over and over again. The question was answered sadly, "No, child. Nicholas can't come to fill your stockings any more." But because they were children and because they had always believed in Nicholas, they had faith that somehow a big heart like his could never die.

A few weeks before Christmas, the villagers met to discuss the matter.

"My little boy, Christian," said one mother sadly, "knows that Nicholas is buried in the pine grove, but he doesn't seem to understand. He believes that Nicholas will come back, and he is determined to hang up his stocking on Christmas Eve, just as he always has."

Kati Dinsler nodded her head. "I feel the same way," she admitted. "It's just that, having known Nicholas, it's impossible to think of Christmas without him."

"The children will have to learn," one father advised, "that if they do hang up their stockings, they will find them empty on Christmas morning." The villagers sat in silence. "Of course," he added slowly, "it wouldn't be fair to Nicholas to allow the children to be disappointed." Each mother and father sat quietly, remembering the joyful Christmas mornings when they were children, and had waked up to find their stockings stuffed with toys and goodies.

"He was a fine, good man," they all agreed. "We must not let the children lose faith in Nicholas."

So that Christmas Eve each child was allowed to hang his stocking from the mantel above the fireplace, and a fire was kept burning warmly on each hearth, in memory of an old and beloved friend whom the children still believed in.

Christmas morning dawned bright and clear. The air was pure and fresh, and the snow lay glistening along the doorways. The little village lay peaceful in the early morning quiet.

Suddenly one door burst open, and with a wild shout little Christian dashed out into the snow. "Look at my stocking! It's filled, just the same as always. Look, everybody, Nicholas did come! Wake up, wake up!"

The children leaped from their beds right into the largest piles of toys they had ever seen, all around the fireplaces and heaped up on the tables and chairs. The bells pealed out a joyful, merry sound. And the happy villagers called to one another in the clear, cold air, "Merry Christmas, Merry Christmas to you! Merry Christmas!"

ISBN 141203865-0